For Tanja and Monika

First paperback edition for the United States and the Philippines published in 2007 by Barron's Educational Series, Inc.

First edition for the United States and the Phillipines copyright © 2002 by Barron's Educational Series, Inc.

The Kiss That Missed was first published in 2002 by Hodder Children's Books.
Copyright © David Melling 2002

The right of David Melling to be identified as the author and illustrator
of this Work has been asserted by him.

All inquiries should be addressed to:
Barron's Educational Series, Inc.
250 Wireless Boulevard
Hauppauge, New York 11788
www.barronseduc.com

Library of Congress Catalog Control Number: 2001090866

ISBN-13: 978-0-7641-3624-5
ISBN-10: 0-7641-3624-0

Date of manufacture : October 2010
Manufactured by : Shenzhen Wing King Tong Paper Products Co. Ltd.,
Shenzhen, Guangdong, China

Printed in China
9 8 7 6 5 4 3

THE KISS
THAT MISSED

WRITTEN AND ILLUSTRATED BY

DAVID MELLING

BARRON'S

ONCE UPON A
Tuesday the King was
in a hurry as usual.
"Goodnight," he said and
blew his son a
Royal Kiss.

It missed.

The young prince watched it rattle around the room,
then bounce out of the window and into the night.

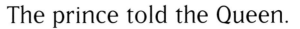

The prince told the Queen.

The Queen told the King,
and the King had a quick
word with his loyal Knight.

"Follow that Kiss!"
he squawked.

The Knight mounted his horse . . .

. . . eventually . . .

and galloped off in hot pursuit until
they came to the wild wood.

Wild creatures with wild eyes, too much
hair, and very bad manners lived here.

It was dark.
It was smelly.
It was . . .

. . . snowing.

They were not alone.

There were bears with long claws
and growly roars, swooping owls
of all shapes and sizes,

and a pack of hungry wolves with
dribbly mouths.

"EEK!"
squeaked the Knight.
And then, suddenly . . .

... with a sparkle the Royal Kiss came floating

by and, in turn, said goodnight to everyone.

Bears stopped being growly,
Owls stopped being swoopy,
Wolves stopped being dribbly,
And before you could say "Follow that kiss!"
They all settled down for a good night's sleep.

The wrinkly old tree trunk **twitched** . . .

After a while they sat down on a wrinkly old tree trunk to rest.

. . .and slowly rose
into the air. . .

. . . above the woods
and into the clouds.

At last they found themselves staring into a pair of very hairy nostrils.

A dragon with "**this-pair-would-be-nice-on-toast**" eyes leered greedily at them.

Suddenly . . .

. . . with a sparkle the Royal Kiss came floating by and flew right up the dragon's nose.

He sat up, sniffed, and blinked.

Slowly, he opened his mouth,
took a deep breath, and . . .

. . . *sneezed!*

"Hang on!" he said as they tumbled through the trees.
"Come back!" he puffed as he lumbered after them.

"I want to pick you up and . . .

. . . kiss you goodnight."

Slowly they all made their way back to the castle.

That night the prince was happy,

the Queen was happy,

and the King promised to stop
always being in a hurry.

He made sure everyone was comfortable
and slowly read them a bedtime story
from beginning to end . . .

. . . almost.

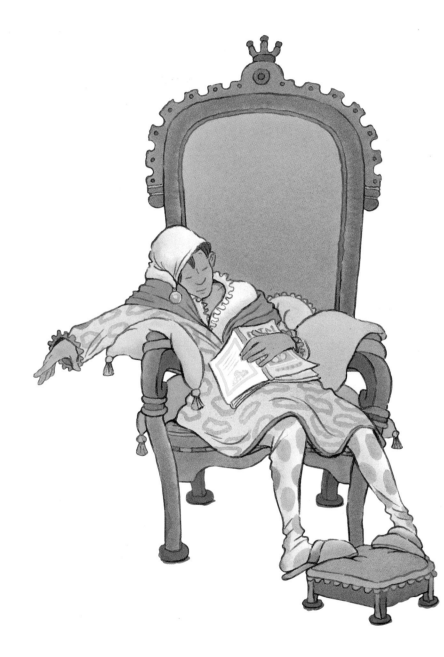